A Honey of a Day

by Janet Marshall

Greenwillow Books, New York

FOR
MY HONEY

The full-color art was created with hand-cut
Pantone papers.
The text type is Gill Sans Bold.

Printed in Hong Kong by South China
Printing Company (1988) Ltd.
First Edition 10 9 8 7 6 5 4 3 2 1

Library of Congress
Cataloging-in-Publication Data

Marshall, Janet Perry.
A honey of a day / by Janet Marshall.
      p.   cm.
Summary: The names and illustrations of many
wildflowers are interwoven into a story about a
woodland wedding.
ISBN 0-688-16917-1
[1. Wildflowers—Fiction.   2. Animals—Fiction.
3. Weddings—Fiction.]   I. Title.
PZ7.M356724Ho   2000   [E]—dc21
98-32207   CIP   AC

On a honey of a day,
in a flowery glade,
a wedding took place in the forest.
Trumpets blared, bluebells rang,
and blue flags waved.

TRUMPET

BLUE FLAG

BLUEBELL

At four-o'clock the guests began
to arrive.
Jack-in-the-pulpit, the preacher,
looking smart in his bishop's cap,
raised his goldenrod to welcome
them.

BISHOP'S CAP

GOLDENROD

JACK-IN-THE-PULPIT

FOUR-
O'CLOCK

Sweet William, the groom, in Dutchman's-breeches held up by red suspenders, waited patiently for the ceremony to begin.

DUTCHMAN'S-BREECHES

SWEET WILLIAM

Along came Johnny-jump-up, the best man. He was turned out in a tuxedo with a bachelor's button pinned to the pocket.

BACHELOR'S BUTTON

JOHNNY-JUMP-UP

LILY OF THE VALLEY

The procession began
with Lily of the valley,
the maid of honor.
She was wearing a cowslip
and a most unusual perfume.

COWSLIP

BLUEBONNET

Pussy willow, the flower girl,
came next, clad in a blue bonnet
and carrying a shepherd's purse.

PUSSY WILLOW

SHEPHERD'S PURSE

JOE-PYE WEED

Then came Joe-pye weed, the ring bearer.
He had forgotten his bow tie
but not his white foxgloves . . .
or the rings, thank goodness.

FOXGLOVE

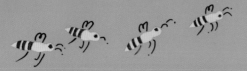

A choir cooed "Here Comes the Bride" softly as a baby's breath.... A buzz went through the air. A radiant black-eyed Susan marched slowly down the aisle. Her gown was made of Queen Anne's lace. She had borrowed lady's slippers, dyed them blue, and put a penny in them. She carried a bouquet of honeycomb.

BLACK-EYED SUSAN

QUEEN ANNE'S LACE

BABY'S BREATH

LADY'S SLIPPER

PASTURE ROSE

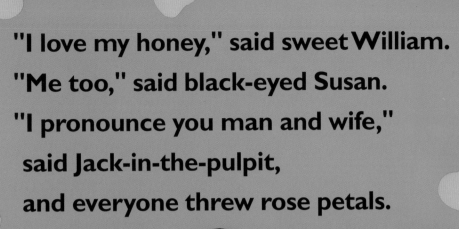

"I love my honey," said sweet William.
"Me too," said black-eyed Susan.
"I pronounce you man and wife,"
said Jack-in-the-pulpit,
and everyone threw rose petals.

WILD POTATO

BUTTER-AND-EGGS

BUTTERCUP

They feasted on
butter-and-eggs,
wild potatoes,
and marshmallows,
and sipped tea
from buttercups.

MARSH MALLOW

Dreaming of a honey moon,
the newlyweds danced
under shooting stars,

SHOOTING STAR

and trumpets blared,
bluebells rang,
and blue flags waved.

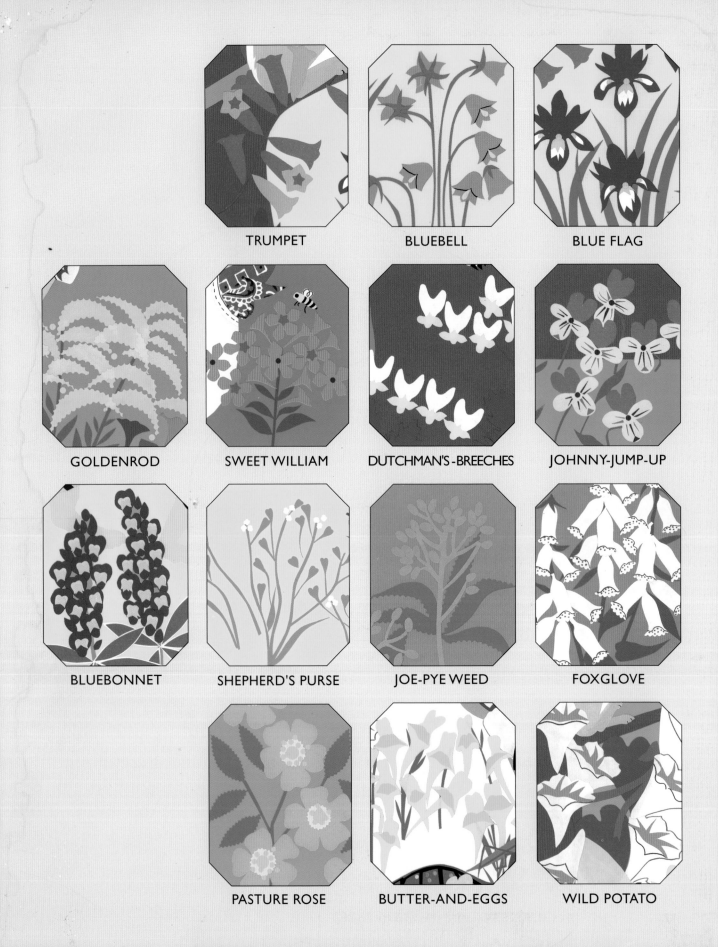

TRUMPET

BLUEBELL

BLUE FLAG

GOLDENROD

SWEET WILLIAM

DUTCHMAN'S-BREECHES

JOHNNY-JUMP-UP

BLUEBONNET

SHEPHERD'S PURSE

JOE-PYE WEED

FOXGLOVE

PASTURE ROSE

BUTTER-AND-EGGS

WILD POTATO

FOUR-O'CLOCK

JACK-IN-THE-PULPIT

BISHOP'S CAP

BACHELOR'S BUTTON

LILY O

PUSSY WILLOW

BABY'S BREATH

LADY'S SLIPPER

MARSH MALLOW